"You're so slow!"
Hare teased Tortoise
one day.

"Yes, but I bet I can beat you in a race," Tortoise laughed.

Hare agreed to the race.

Fox chose the start and the finish line.

Hare and Tortoise started the race together ...

Run Tortoise Run!
Hare

... but Hare was so sure he would win that he lay down to sleep.

Tortoise crawled on until she got to the finish line.

Run tortoise Run
Go Hare!

Then she lay down to sleep.

When Hare woke up, he raced to the finish line …

... but Tortoise was already there!

Run, tortoise Run!

“Tortoise wins!” cried Fox.

1

Puzzle Time!

Put these pictures in the right order and tell the story!

Which words describe Tortoise and which describe Hare?

Turn over for answers!

Notes for adults

TADPOLES are structured to provide support for newly independent readers. The stories may also be used by adults for sharing with young children.

Starting to read alone can be daunting. **TADPOLES** help by providing visual support and repeating words and phrases. These books will both develop confidence and encourage reading and rereading for pleasure.

If you are reading this book with a child, here are a few suggestions:

1. Make reading fun! Choose a time to read when you and the child are relaxed and have time to share the story.
2. Talk about the story before you start reading. Look at the cover and the blurb. What might the story be about? Why might the child like it?
3. Encourage the child to retell the story, using the jumbled picture puzzle as a starting point. Extend vocabulary with the matching words to characters puzzle.
4. Discuss the story and see if the child can relate it to their own experience, and perhaps think about the moral of the fable.
5. Give praise! Remember that small mistakes need not always be corrected.

Answers

Here is the correct order!

1. a 2. e 3. c 4. f 5. d 6. b

Words to describe Hare:
fast, quick

Words to describe Tortoise:
slow, steady